FOAL

ALEXANDER McCALL SMITH

The Great Cake Mystery

Alexander McCall Smith is the author of the No. 1 Ladies' Detective Agency series, the Isabel Dalhousie series, the Portuguese Irregular Verbs series, the 44 Scotland Street series, and the Corduroy Mansions series. He was born in what is now known as Zimbabwe and lives in Scotland, where in his spare time he is a bassoonist in the RTO (Really Terrible Orchestra).

www.alexandermccallsmith.com

The Great
Cake Mystery

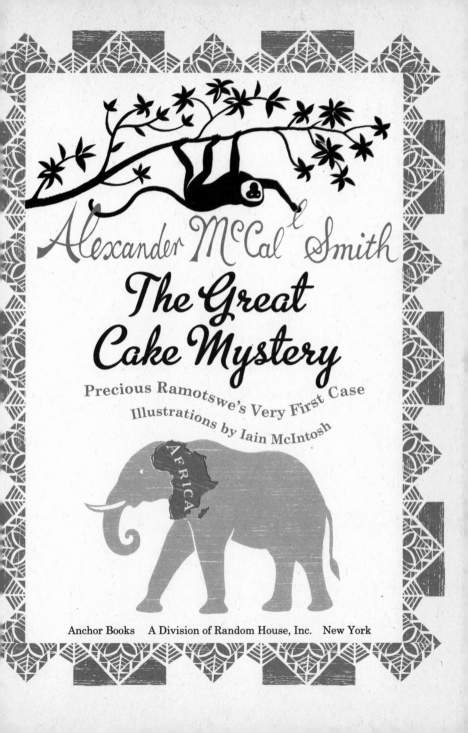

Alexander McCall Smith

The Great Cake Mystery

Precious Ramotswe's Very First Case

Illustrations by Iain McIntosh

Anchor Books   A Division of Random House, Inc.   New York

The Great
Cake Mystery

A MAP OF
BOTSWANA

PULA

KALAHARI
DESERT

BOTSWANA

Francistown

0   miles   100

GABORONE

ave you ever said to yourself, *Wouldn't it be nice to be a detective?* Most of us will never have the chance to make that dream come true. Detectives, you see, are born that way. Right from the beginning they just *know* that this is what they want to be. And right from the beginning they show that solving mysteries is something they can do rather well.

This is the story about a girl who became a detective. Her name was Precious.

Precious smiled a lot. She often smiled even when she was not thinking about anything in particular. Nice people smile a lot,

3

and Precious Ramotswe was one of the nicest girls in Botswana. Everyone said so.

Botswana was the country she lived in.
It was down toward the bottom of Africa.

She lived in a wide dry land, which had a lot of amazing things to see.

There was the Kalahari Desert, a great stretch of dry grass and thorn trees that went on and on into the distance, farther than any eye can see. Then there was the great river in the north, which flowed the wrong way. It did not flow into the ocean, as rivers usually do, but back into the heart of Africa. When it reached the sands of the Kalahari, it drained away, just like water disappears down the drain of a bath.

But most interesting, of course, were the wild animals. There were many of these in Botswana: lions, elephants, leopards, monkeys—the list goes on. Precious had not seen all of these animals, but she had heard about most of them. Her father, a kind man

5

whose name was Obed, often spoke about them, and she loved the tales he told.

"Tell me about the time you were nearly eaten by a lion," she would ask. And Obed, who had told her that story perhaps a hundred times before, would tell her again. And it was every bit as exciting each time he told it.

"I was a young man then," he began.

"How young?" asked Precious.

"About eighteen, I think," he said. "I went up north to see my uncle, who lived way out in the country, or the bush as we call it in Africa, very far from everywhere."

"Did anybody else live there?" asked Precious. She was always asking questions, which was a sign that she might become a good detective. Do you like to ask questions? Many people who ask lots of questions become detectives, because that is what detectives do. They ask a lot of questions.

"It was a very small village," Obed said. "It was just a few huts, really, and a fenced place where they kept the cattle. They had this fence, you see, which protected the cattle from the lions at night."

This fence had to be quite strong. A few strands of wire cannot keep lions out.

That is hopeless when it comes to lions—
they would just knock down such a fence
with a single blow of their paw. A proper
lion fence has to be made of strong poles,
from the trunks of trees.

"So there I was," Obed said. "I had gone to
spend a few days with my uncle and his family. They were good to me and I liked my cous-
ins. There were six of them—four boys and
two girls. We had many adventures together.

"I slept in one of the huts with three
of the boys. We did not have beds in those
days—we had sleeping mats made out of
reeds, which we laid out on the floor of the
hut. They were nice to sleep on. They were
much cooler than a bed and blankets in the
hot weather, and easier to store too."

Precious was quiet now. This was the part of the story that she liked the best.

"And then," her father said, "and then one night I woke up to a strange sound. It was like the sound a large pig will make when it's sniffing about for food, only a little bit quieter."

"Did you know what it was?" she asked, holding her breath as she waited for her

father to reply. She knew what the answer would be, of course. She had heard the story so many times. But it was always exciting, always enough to keep you sitting on the very edge of your seat.

He shook his head. "No, I didn't. And that was why I thought I should go outside and find out."

Precious closed her eyes tight. She could hardly bear to hear what was coming.

"It was a lion," her father said. "And he was right outside the hut, standing there,

looking at me from underneath his great
dark mane."

CHAPTER TWO

Precious opened her eyes cautiously, one at a time, just in case there was a lion in the room. But there was just her father, telling his story.

"How did that lion get in?" she asked. "How did he get past that big strong fence?"

Obed shook his head. "Somebody had not closed the gate properly," he said. "It was carelessness."

What would you do if you found yourself face to face with a great lion? Perhaps you would just close your eyes and hope that you were dreaming—that is what Obed did when he saw the terrifying lion star-

13

ing straight at him. But when he opened his eyes again, the lion was still there, and worse still, was beginning to open its great mouth.

Precious caught her breath. "Did you see his teeth?" she asked.

Obed nodded. "The moonlight was very bright," he said. "His big teeth were white and sharp."

Precious shuddered and listened intently as her father explained what happened next.

Obed turned his head very slowly. He could not get back to the hut. It would take him too close to the beast. But, just a few steps away, were the family's grain bins. These were like garden pots—but much big-

ger—that were used for storing corn. They were made out of pressed mud, baked hard by the hot sun, and they were very strong.

"I ran—not back to the hut, but to the nearest grain bin. I pushed the cover back and jumped in, bringing the lid down on top of my head. I was safe! Or so I thought."

Precious breathed a sigh of relief.

"There was very little grain left in that bin," Obed said. "So there was plenty of room for me to crouch down."

"And spiders too?" asked Precious, with a shudder.

"There are always spiders in grain bins," said Obed. "But it wasn't spiders I was worried about."

"It was—"

Obed finished the sentence for her. "Yes, it was the lion. I could hear him outside, scratching and snuffling at the lid.

"I knew that it would only be a matter of time before he pushed the lid off with one of his big paws, and I knew that I had to do something. But what could I do?

"So I took a handful of those dusty husks and then, pushing up the lid a tiny bit, I tossed them straight into the face of the lion."

Precious looked at her father wide-eyed. This was the best part of the story.

"And what did he do?" she asked.

Obed smiled. "He breathed them in and then he gave the loudest, most powerful sneeze that has ever been sneezed in Botswana, or possibly in all Africa. Ka . . . chow!

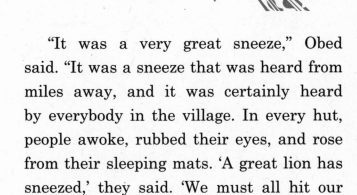

"It was a very great sneeze," Obed said. "It was a sneeze that was heard from miles away, and it was certainly heard by everybody in the village. In every hut, people awoke, rubbed their eyes, and rose from their sleeping mats. 'A great lion has sneezed,' they said. 'We must all hit our pots and pans as hard as we can. That will frighten him away.'

"And that is what happened. As the

people began to strike their pots and pans with spoons and forks, the lion tucked his tail between his legs and ran off into the bush. He was not frightened of eating one unlucky young man, but even he could not stand up to a whole village of people all pounding on pots. Lions do not like that sort of noise."

"I am glad that you were not eaten by that lion," Precious said.

"And so am I," Obed said.

"Because if the lion had eaten you, I would never have been born," Precious said.

"And if you had never been born, then I would never have been able to get to know the brightest and nicest girl in all Botswana," said her father.

Precious thought for a moment. "So it would have been a bad thing for both of us."

"Yes," said Obed. "And maybe a bad thing for the lion too."

"Oh, why was that?"

"Because I might have given him indigestion," said Obed. "It's well known that if a lion eats a person who's feeling cross at the time, he gets indigestion."

Precious was not sure whether this was true, or whether he was just making it up to amuse her. She decided that it was not true and told him so.

He smiled and looked at her in a curious way. "You can tell when people are making things up, can't you?"

Precious nodded. She thought that was probably right—she *could* tell.

"Perhaps you will become a detective one day," he said.

CHAPTER THREE

When her father said to her that one day she might become a detective, she at first thought, *What a strange idea*, but then she asked herself, *Why not?* "Yes, I could be a detective," Precious said. "But surely it will be years and years before I get a case."

She was wrong about that. A case came up sooner than she thought it would. Detectives say their first case is always the hardest. Well, Precious was not sure if that was true for her, but her first case was certainly not easy. This is what happened.

The school Precious went to was on a hill. This meant that the children had a long

21

climb in the mornings, but it was a wonderful place for their lessons. Looking out of the windows, they could gaze out to where other little hills popped up like rocks in a stream. And you could hear sounds from far away too—the tinkling of cattle bells, the rumbling of thunder far off in the distance, the cry of a hawk soaring in the wind.

It was, as you can imagine, a very happy  school. The teachers were happy to be working in such a nice town, the children were happy to have kind teachers who did not shout at them, and even the school

cat, who had a comfortable den outside, was happy with the mice that could be chased. But then something happened.

What happened was that there was a thief. Now, most people don't steal things. Most people know you should not take things that belong to others. For many of us, that is Rule Number One.

RULE NUMBER ONE
Don't help yourself to other people's things!

So, a thief . . . and a thief at school too!

The first person to notice what was going on was Tapiwa (TAP-EE-WAH) a girl in the same class as Precious.

TAP•EE•WAH

"Do you know what?" she whispered to Precious as they walked home after school one afternoon.

"No," said Precious. "What?"

"There must be a thief at school," Tapiwa said, looking over her shoulder in case anybody heard what she had to say. "I brought a piece of cake to school with me this morning. I left it in my bag in the hall-way outside the classroom." She paused. "I was really looking forward to eating it at break-time."

"I love cake," Precious said. She closed her eyes and thought of some of the cakes she enjoyed. Cakes with thick icing. Cakes with jam on top of them. Cakes sprinkled with sugar and then dipped in little colored sugarballs. There were so many cakes . . . and all of them were so delicious.

"Somebody took my cake," Tapiwa complained. "I had wrapped it in a small piece of paper. Well, it was gone, and I found the paper lying on the floor."

Precious frowned. "Gone?"

"Eaten up," said Tapiwa. "There were crumbs on the floor and little bits of icing. I picked them up and tasted them. I could tell that they came from my cake."

"Did you tell the teacher?" asked Precious.

Her friend sighed. "Yes," she said. "But I don't think that she believed me. She said, 'Are you sure you didn't forget that you ate it?' She said that this sometimes happened. People ate a piece of cake and then forgot that they had done so."

Precious looked at Tapiwa. Was she the sort of person to eat a piece of cake and then forget all about it? She did not think so.

"It was stolen," Tapiwa said. "That's what happened. There's a thief in the school. Who do you think it is?"

"I don't know," Precious said. She found it hard to imagine any member of their class doing something like that. Everybody seemed so honest. And yet, when you came to think of it, if there were grown-up thieves, then those thieves must have been children once, and perhaps they were already thieves even when they were young. Or did people only become thieves a bit later on? It was a very interesting question, and she would have to think about it a bit more. Which was what she did as she walked home that day, under that high, hot African sun. She thought about thieves and what a detective would do about them.

he might easily have forgotten all about it—after all, it was only a piece of cake—but the next day it happened again. This time it was a piece of bread that was stolen—not an ordinary piece of bread, though: this one was covered in delicious strawberry jam. You can lose a plain piece of bread and not think twice about it, but when you lose one spread thickly with strawberry jam it's an altogether more serious matter.

The owner of this piece of bread (with jam) was a boy called Sepo. Everybody liked this boy because he had a habit of saying

funny things. If somebody can say something funny, then that often makes everybody feel happy.

If you saw such a piece of bread sitting on a plate your mouth would surely begin to water. And yes, you might imagine how delicious it would

taste. But would you really eat it if you knew it belonged to somebody else? Of course not.

It happened at lunchtime. Every day, at twelve o'clock precisely, the school cook, a very large lady called Big Mrs. Molipi (MO–LEE–PEE), would bang a saucepan with a

MO•LEE•PEE

ladle. This was the signal for all the children to sit down on the porch and wait to be given a plate of food that she had cooked with her assistant and cousin. This assistant was called Not-so-Big Mrs. Molipi, and, as the name tells us, she was much smaller than the chief cook herself. "Time for lunch!" Big Mrs. Molipi shouted in her very loud voice.

Then Not-so-Big Mrs. Molipi shouted, in a much smaller, squeakier voice, "Time for lunch!"

Big Mrs. Molipi's food was all right, but

just all right. It was, in fact, a bit boring, since she only had one recipe, it seemed, which was a sort of paste made out of corn and served with green peas and mashed turnips.

"It's very healthy," said Big Mrs. Molipi. "So stop complaining, children, and eat up!"

"Yes," said Not-so-Big Mrs. Molipi. "So stop complaining, children, and eat up!"

Not-so-Big Mrs. Molipi did not say any-thing other than what she heard her larger cousin say. She thought it was safer that way. If you said anything new, she imagined, then people could look at you, and Not-so-Big Mrs. Molipi did not like the thought of that.

It was no surprise that many of the chil-

dren liked to make lunch a little bit more interesting by bringing their own food. Some brought a bit of fruit, or a sugar doughnut, or perhaps a cookie. Then, after lunch, when they all had a bit of free time before going back into the classroom, they would eat these special treats.

Sepo had brought his piece of bread and jam in a brown paper bag. While Big Mrs. Molipi served lunch, he had left the bag in the classroom, tucked away safely under his desk. He was sure that this was where he had left it, and so when he went back in and saw that it had disappeared he was very surprised indeed.

"My bread!" he wailed. "Somebody's taken my bread!"

Precious was walking past the open door of the classroom when she heard this. She looked in: there was Sepo standing miserably by his desk.

"Are you sure?" Precious asked.

"Of course I'm sure," Sepo said. "It was

there when we went out for lunch. Now it isn't, and *I* didn't take it."

Precious walked into the classroom and stared at the spot being pointed out by Sepo. There was certainly nothing there.

"I'll ask people if they saw anything," she said, thinking that she may have found her first case. "In the meantime, you can have half of my biscuit. I hope that will make you feel better."

It did. Sepo was still upset, but not quite as upset as he had been when he made the discovery.

"What do you think happened?"

"I don't know, it's mysterious," she said and thought how fun mysteries were.

"There must be a thief in the school," Sepo said as they walked out into the play-ground. "Who do you think it is, Precious?"

Precious shrugged. "I just don't know," she said. "It could be . . ." She paused. "It could be anyone."

"I think I may know who it is," he said. He did not speak very loudly, even though there was nobody else about.

Precious asked, "How do you know that? Did you see somebody taking it?"

Sepo again looked over his shoulder. "No," he said. "I didn't see anybody actually take it. But I did see somebody walking away from the classroom door."

Precious held her breath, waiting for Sepo to say more. He stayed silent, though, and so she whispered to him, "Who?"

Sepo did not say anything, but after hesitating for a moment or two he very carefully pointed to somebody standing in the playground.

"Him," he whispered. "It's him. I saw him."

That night, as Precious lay on her sleeping mat, waiting for her father to come in and tell her a story—as he always did—she thought about what happened at school. She did not like the thought of there being a thief at school—thieves spoiled everything. They made people suspicious of one another, which was not a good thing at all. People should be able to trust other people, without worrying about whether they will steal their possessions.

But even if she did not like the thought of there being a thief, neither did she like the

39

thought that an innocent person might be suspected. She did not know the boy whom Sepo had pointed out—she had seen him, of course, and she knew his name, Poloko (PO–LOW–KO), but she did not know very much about him. And she certainly did not know that he was a thief.

Poloko was a rather round boy.

PO·LOW·KO

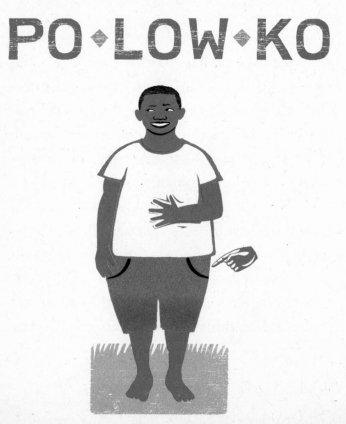

If you saw him walking along the street, you might think that perhaps that was a boy who ate a little bit too much. And if you got to know him a bit better, then you might be sure that this was so and that those bulges in his pockets were indeed sweets—a lot of them.

But just because somebody has lots of sweets does *not* mean that he has stolen them. One thing, you see, does not always lead to another. That is something that all detectives learn very early in their career.

The next day at school, when they were copying out letters from the board, Sepo whispered, "Have you told anybody about the thief?"

Precious shook her head. "We don't know who it is. How can I tell the teacher about something I don't know?"

"But *I* know who it is," Sepo said. "And Big Mrs. Molipi told me that somebody has stolen three iced buns from her kitchen! She told me that this morning. Poloko's probably eaten them already!"

Precious listened in silence. She thought that this was a very unfair thing to say and she was about to tell Sepo so when the teacher gave them a stern look. So Precious just said, "Shh!" instead and left it at that. But later, when the children were let out to play while the teachers drank their tea, Sepo and Tapiwa came up to her and said they wanted to speak to her.

"Are you going to help us deal with the thief?" Tapiwa said.

Precious tried to look surprised. She knew what they meant, but she did not want to help them without any proof. "I don't know what you're talking about," she said. "How can we deal with the thief if we don't know who it is?"

"But we do know," Sepo said. "It's Poloko, that's who it is."

Precious stared at Sepo. "You don't know that," she said. "So I'm not going to help you until you have some proof."

Sepo smiled. "All right," he said. "If you want some proof, we'll get it for you. We're going to look at his hands."

Precious wondered what he meant by that, but before she had the time to ask him, Sepo and Tapiwa ran off to the other side of the playground where Poloko was sitting on a rock. Precious ran behind them—not because she wanted to help them, but because she wanted to see what was happening.

"Hold out your hands," Tapiwa said to Poloko. "Come on. Hold them out."

Poloko was surprised, but held out his hands. Tapiwa bent down to examine them.

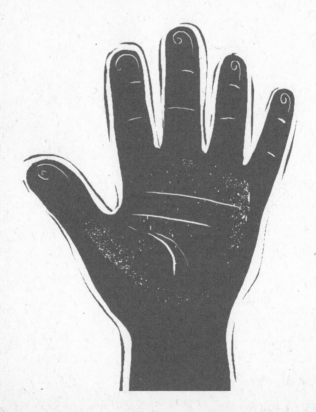

After a few moments, she pointed out something to Sepo, and he also bent down to look. Then Tapiwa reached out to feel Poloko's hands.

"Hah!" she shouted. "It's just as we thought. Your hands are sticky!"

Poloko tried to say something, but his words were drowned out by the shouts of

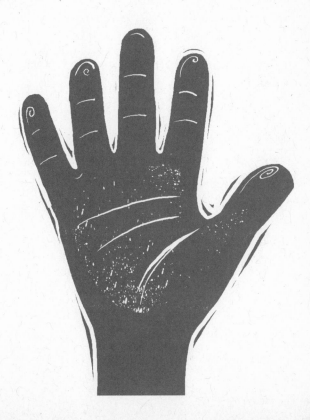

Tapiwa and Sepo. "Thief!" they cried out. "Thief! Thief!" It was a shrill cry, and it chilled Precious's blood just to hear it. Precious wondered what it would be like to hear somebody shout that about you—especially if you were not a thief and never had been.

Precious stood quite still. The others were now making such a noise that one of the teachers was coming to see what was wrong.

"What's all this noise?" the teacher asked. "Can't you children play quietly?"

"We've found the thief," Tapiwa shouted. "Look, Mma, look! His hands are covered in stickiness. If you want to know where those iced buns are, they're right there—in Poloko's stomach!"

hat's all this?" she asked. "Are you children fighting?"

"We're not fighting, Mma," cried Tapiwa, pointing a finger at Poloko. "We've found the thief. It's this boy! This boy right here!"

The teacher looked at Poloko. "Have you stolen something, Poloko?"

Poloko hung his head. "No, Mma, I have not stolen anything."

The teacher turned to stare at Tapiwa and Sepo. "Why do you say he's a thief?"

"Because some iced buns have been eaten," Sepo blurted out. "And his hands are sticky. Look at them, Mma!"

47

The teacher sighed. "Lots of people have sticky hands," she said. "That doesn't mean that they're thieves." She paused, looking down at Poloko." You're sure you haven't stolen anything, Poloko?"

The boy was close to crying. "I have not stolen anything, Mma. I promise you."

The teacher shook a finger at Tapiwa and Sepo. "You be careful about accusing people of things when you have no proof," she said. "Now everybody go off and play and no more trouble, please."

Tapiwa and Sepo walked off, but only after throwing a disapproving look at Poloko. It was a look that said, *You're still a thief, you know*. And Poloko, who was clearly feeling very miserable, walked off in the other direction.

Precious waited for a moment before following the dejected-looking boy. "Poloko," she said as she caught up with him. "I believe you. I don't think you're a thief."

He stopped. "Thank you, Precious. I know you don't think that." He paused, looking over his shoulder to where the other children were standing, listening to Tapiwa and Sepo. "But they'll all think I'm a thief."

Precious knew that what he said was true. But she did not like to think that he was still unhappy, and so she tried to comfort him further. "It doesn't matter what people like that think," she said. "What matters is what your friends think. I'm your friend, and I know that you're telling the truth."

He listened to what she said and was about to say something when the bell sounded for them to return to the classroom. So he simply muttered, "Thank you."

That afternoon, when all the children left the school and began to walk back home under the hot African sun, Precious found Poloko and asked him to walk with her.

He was pleased that she asked, as they could both see the other children looking at him suspiciously.

"You see," he said. "They've told everybody. Now they all think I'm a thief."

"Pay no attention to them," Precious said. "They can think what they like."

She knew, though, that it was not that simple. All of us worry about what other people think, even if we do not have to. It was easy to tell somebody to ignore that sort of thing; it was much harder to put such advice into practice.

They set off, following the path down the hill. It was a narrow path and a winding one—here and there were great boulders—and the path twisted around them. There were trees in between the boulders, and their roots had worked their way through gaps in the stone. These trees made the places in between the rocks a cool refuge from the heat of the sun, and Precious and Poloko sat down to rest on their way home.

There was a noise off among the rocks, and they both gave a start.

"A snake!" whispered Poloko.

 snake," said Poloko.

"Perhaps," Precious said. "Should we look?"

Poloko nodded. "Yes, but we must be careful."

They heard the noise again. This time Precious thought that it might have come from the tree, and she looked up into the branches.

"There!" she said, pointing into the tangle of leaves and branches.

Poloko looked up. He expected to see a snake wound around one of the branches, but that was not what he spotted.

53

"Monkeys!" he said.

Precious smiled. "They were watching us."

And then, just as she spoke, one of the monkeys dropped something. It fell down from the tree and landed on a sunny patch of ground. Poloko watched it and then ran forward to pick it up, paying no heed to the excited chattering of the monkeys above his head.

For a moment or two he stared at it before passing it to Precious.

It was a piece of iced bun.

Now she was sure Poloko was not the thief. But it was one thing to be sure about something and quite another to prove it to others. That is something that all detectives know. Although she had only started being

a detective, Precious was well aware that you had to be able to show people something if you wanted them to believe it.

That night, as she lay on her sleeping mat, she went over in her mind what she had seen. The monkeys were the culprits— they had given themselves away—but it would not be easy to catch them in the act. Monkeys were very quick and, in their own special monkeyish way, very cunning. It was much easier to catch a human being than to catch a monkey.

She closed her eyes and imagined how monkeys would steal buns. They would dart in through the window when nobody was looking and their little hands—so like human hands in every respect, but a bit hairier—would stretch out and snatch.

She settled down and closed her eyes. It took some time for her to drop off, as it often did when she was thinking about a mystery, but eventually she became drowsier and drowsier and went to sleep.

She dreamed and of course her dreams were about monkeys. She was walking under some trees in her dream, and the monkeys were up in the branches above her. They were calling out and, to her surprise, they were calling her name. *Come up here, Precious. Come up here and join us.*

In your dreams you can often do things that you just cannot do when you are awake. Precious couldn't normally climb trees very well, but in her dreams she could. It was very easy, in fact, and within moments she was up in the branches with the monkeys. They gathered about her, their tiny, wizened faces filled with joy at finding a new friend. Soft, tiny hands touched her, stroking her gently, while other hands explored her ears and hair.

Then they took her by the hand and led her along one of the branches. The ground was far below, and hard and rocky. *Don't be frightened,* said one of the monkeys. *It's very easy, you know.*

And with that, Precious began to swing from branch to branch, just as the monkeys did. It was the most wonderful, light feeling, and her heart soared as she moved effortlessly through the canopy of leaves. So this was what it was like to live in the trees—it

was like living in the sky. And it was like flying too. As she let go of one branch and swung through the air to another, she felt as light as a leaf itself might feel as it dropped from a bough.

She moved through the trees, the monkeys all about her, waving to her with their little hands, encouraging her. And then slowly the trees thinned out and she was on the ground again. She looked for her friends, the monkeys, and saw that they were gone.

Those little hands . . . What if the thing they were trying to snatch was even stickier than the stickiest of iced buns?

Like all good ideas, it was enough to make you sit bolt upright. And that was what Precious did, her eyes wide, a broad

smile on her face. Yes! The dream had shown her. She had worked out how to trap a thief, particularly one with tiny hands!

The next morning, Precious was the first
in the house to get out of bed. She had
work to do—detective work—and her first
task was to bake a cake. This was not difficult, as she was a good cook and had a well-
tried recipe for sponge cake. Precious had
learned to cook because she had to—her
mother died when she was very small—and,
although her father thought he was looking
after her, when it came to cooking meals
Precious looked after him!

The cake did not take long and was soon
out of the oven. It smelled delicious, but she
resisted the temptation to cut a slice for her-

self and try it. Rather than doing that, she took a knife and cut out the middle of the cake so that it was left with a large hole in it.

The next bit of the plan was more difficult. Her father had a workshop next to the house—a place where he fixed fence posts and did odd carpentry jobs for friends. On a shelf in this workshop was a large pot of glue that he used for sticking wood together—it was very strong glue, a thick, sticky paste.

Very carefully, making sure to get none on her fingers, Precious ladled out several spoonfuls of this glue onto a plate. After replacing the glue-pot on the shelf, she went back to the kitchen. Now she took the piece of cake that she had cut from the center and mixed it up with the glue. It made a wonderfully sticky mess—just the thing she was looking for.

She then put this sticky mixture back in the hole in the cake and covered the whole thing with icing. For good measure, she stuck a few red and yellow jelly sweets on the top. Nobody will be able to resist such a cake, she thought. Certainly no monkey could.

"That's a nice cake you've cooked," her father said over breakfast. "Is that for your teacher?"

Precious smiled. "No, I don't think so." She could imagine what would happen if the teacher ate that particular cake.

"For your friends?" asked her father.

Precious thought for a moment. She remembered her dream and the way the monkeys in it had welcomed her to their trees. Yes, they were her friends, she thought. In spite of all their tricks and their mischievousness, they were her friends.

She carried the cake to school in a box. When she arrived, she put the box down carefully and took out its mouthwatering contents.

"Look at that cake!" shouted somebody.

"Don't leave it there," said another. "If you leave it there, Precious, then Poloko will be sure to steal it!"

Other children laughed at this, but Precious did not. "Don't say that," she said crossly. But they said it again.

"Poloko will eat that entirely up," one of the boys said. "That's why he's so fat. He's a fat thief!"

Precious hoped that Poloko had not

heard this, but she feared that he had. She saw Poloko walking away, his head lowered. People were so unkind, she thought. How would they like to be called a thief? Well, she would show them just how wrong they were.

With the cake left outside, on the shelf where the children left their bags, school began. Precious walked into the classroom and tried to concentrate on the lesson that the teacher was giving, but it was not easy. Her mind kept wandering, and she found herself imagining what was going on outside. The cake was sitting there, the perfect temptation for any passing monkey, and it could only be a question of time before . . .

It happened suddenly. One moment everything was quiet, and the next there came a great squealing sound from outside. The squealing became louder and was soon a sort of howling sound, rather like the siren of a fire engine.

The teacher and the entire class looked up in astonishment.

"What on earth is going on?" asked the teacher. "Open the door, Sepo, and see what's happening."

The entire class took this as an invitation to go to the door, and they were soon all gathered round the open door and the windows too, peering out to see what was going on.

What was happening was that two monkeys were dancing up and down alongside the shelf, their hands stuck firmly in the mixture of glue and cake. Struggle as they might to free themselves, each time they pulled out a hand a long strand of glue dragged it back in. They were thoroughly and completely stuck to the cake.

"See," shouted Precious in triumph. "There are the thieves. See there!"

The teacher laughed. "Well, well. So it's

monkeys who have been up to no good. Well, well!"

The school gardener had been alerted by the sound of squealing, and he now appeared. Seizing the monkeys, he pulled them away from the cake, freeing them to scamper back to the trees not far away.

"Little rascals," he shouted, shaking a fist at them as they disappeared into the trees.

The teacher called everybody back to their desks. "We shall have to be more careful in the future," she said. "Don't leave anything out to tempt those monkeys. That's the way to deal with that."

Precious said nothing.

Then the teacher continued. "And I hope that some of you have learned a lesson," she said. "Those who accused Poloko of being

a thief may like to think about what they have just seen."

The teacher looked at Sepo and Tapiwa, who both looked down at the floor. Precious watched them. They had learned a lesson, she thought.

Later, on the way back from school, Poloko came up to her and thanked her for what she had done. "You are a very kind girl," he said. "Thank you."

"That's all right," she said.

"You're going to be a very good detective one day. Do you still want to be one?"

She thought for a moment. It was a good thing to be a detective. You could help people who needed help. You could make people happier—as Poloko now was.

"Yes," she said. "I think I do."

They walked on. In the trees not far away,

there were some small eyes watching them from the leaves. The monkeys. Her friends.

Poloko walked her to her house, and Precious turned to him and said, "Would you like me to make a cake? We could eat it for our tea."

He said he would, and while Precious baked the cake, he sat outside and sniffed the delicious smell wafting through the kitchen window.

Then the cake was ready, and they each had a large slice.

"Perfect," Poloko said. "First-class, number one cake."

And that was when she thought, *When I have a detective agency, I'll call it the No. 1 Ladies' Detective Agency.*

Many years later, she did just that.

Alexander McCall Smith

Dear Reader,

There are some stories that an author feels he or she just has to write, and for me this story of the early life of my Botswana heroine, Precious Ramotswe, is one.

Over the decade or so since the No. 1 Ladies' Detective Agency books have been widely available, I have been struck by the number of young people who have engaged with the story of this rather amiable African woman who starts a tiny detective agency and who devotes herself to helping people with their personal problems. I have also been struck by the extent to which the books were shared within families; it not being uncommon for grandparents, parents, and children all to take turns in reading the latest installment of Mma Ramotswe's story. This pleased me greatly, as reading the same book is a good way of binding generations together. At the same time, even if a young child is a strong reader, these books could pose a bit of a challenge—hence the idea of writing something that could be appreciated by readers under ten, while at the same time being, I hope, an entertaining read for all ages. I know I have a lot of fans who are teachers and librarians and hope that the book will also appeal to them as one they can share and use with younger readers.

It also seemed to me that it would be an intriguing and enjoyable thing to imagine the life of Precious when she was a young girl. If it is true that we often manifest at a very early age those qualities and interests that will determine what we do in later life, then it is reasonable to think that the young Precious Ramotswe was a bit of a detective all along. So the story emerged of Precious dealing with a mystery that arises in her class at school. And of course the issues that arise in that context are the same as those that arise in an adult mystery: honesty and dishonesty, friendship, suspicion, and so on. But, I hope that this book is able to do a little bit more. I hope that it gives the young reader something of the flavor of Africa and will inspire them to read more about that wonderful continent and its remarkable people.

—Alexander McCall Smith

CHARACTER GUIDE

Precious Ramotswe (RAM-OTS-WE)—She smiles a lot and is one of the nicest girls in Botswana. Precious asks a lot of questions and can always tell when people are making things up.

Obed Ramotswe—Precious's father, he is a kind man who tells great stories. Obed was almost eaten by a lion when he was young.

Tapiwa (TAP-EE-WAH)—a girl who is Precious's classmate. She is the first to realize that there is a thief at their school.

Sepo—One of Precious's classmates whom everyone likes and has a habit of saying funny things.

Big Mrs. Molipi (MO-LEE-PEE)—the school cook, a very large lady who seems to only know one recipe.

Not-so-Big Mrs. Molipi—Big Mrs. Molipi's assistant and cousin. She is much smaller than her cousin.

Poloko (PO-LOW-KO)—a rather round boy who is Precious's classmate. He walks around with sweets in his pockets and everyone thinks he is the cake thief.

GEOGRAPHY AND PEOPLE OF BOTSWANA

Botswana is located towards the bottom of Africa and is roughly the size of Texas. It is a wide dry land with lots of amazing things to see. The capital is Gaborone. Pronounced Ha-bo-ro-nee.

Setswana is the language spoken in most of Botswana. Most people also speak English and newspapers, for example, will be in both languages.

The Kalahari is a semi-desert, which occupies the central and western parts of Botswana. It is a great stretch of dry grass and thorn trees where very few people live.

The Bush—the rural, undeveloped land of Botswana, which is far from civilization.

Okavango—the great river in the north that flows the wrong way—instead of flowing from land to sea, the water goes from the ocean to the heart of Africa where it is absorbed into the sands of the Kalahari.

Wildlife—Botswana has a wide variety of wild animals, including lions, elephants, zebras, buffalo, leopards, hippos, hyenas, baboons, snakes, monkeys, and many more.

Mma is the term used to address a woman, and may be placed before her name. It is pronounced "ma" (with a long *a*). This is what Precious and her classmates call their teacher.

READER'S GUIDE

ABOUT THE BOOK:

It sometimes happens that a person's true profession becomes apparent even in childhood ... and that is the case for Precious Ramotswe. In this, her very first detective case, Precious exhibits the character traits that will contribute to her future success as an adult. At the same time, she is able to make a new friend and prevent a terrible injustice in the schoolyard. Set in her beloved homeland of Botswana, the story introduces readers to the culture and topography of the country.

BOOK TALK:

Food is disappearing from a school in Botswana. Not just any food, but the most delicious, sweet, lovely desserts that students are bringing as a treat for themselves after they eat the healthy but boring lunches provided for them at school. The children whose sweets have been stolen quickly point a finger at one of their less popular classmates, but Precious Ramotswe does not believe anyone in her school could be a thief, and she sets out to solve the mystery. See if you can figure out the clues along with Precious as you read the story of her very first detective case.

PRE-READING ACTIVITY:

1. Locate the country of Botswana on a map of Africa. Divide your group into teams to learn about the geography, wildlife, customs, economy, and education system of Botswana; then share what you have learned with others in the group.

DISCUSSION QUESTIONS:

1. Do you agree with the author's statement that detectives are "born that way"?

2. Why does the author stress that Precious is a "nice" person? What personality traits do you think a nice person should possess?

3. Discuss the significance of Obed's story about the lion. What does it tell Precious about her father? Why does she like to hear the story over and over?

4. How does Precious know which parts of the lion story are true and which parts are stretching the truth? Why is this important?

5. Why does Tapiwa tell Precious about the cake thief? Why does she assume that the thief is someone in the school?

6. Precious wonders if people who grow up to steal were thieves when they were children or if they became thieves later on. This question is not answered in the book. What do you think?

7. Why does everyone like Sepo? What qualities does he have that make him popular with the other students?

8. Why do Sepo and Tapiwa believe that Poloko is the thief? What evidence do they have? Why are the other children so quick to believe that Poloko is the thief?

9. How does Poloko feel when the others accuse him of stealing the food? How would you feel if you were accused of something that you didn't do? Why is it so hard for Poloko to defend himself?

10. Why does Precious believe Poloko is innocent? Why does she tell him she will be his friend when everyone else believes the worst about him?

11. How do Precious and Poloko discover the real thieves? If they had not walked home from school together, taking their time, would they have solved the mystery?

12. Solving the mystery is one thing, but the real challenge is proving it to the others. How does Precious convince the other children and the teacher of the truth? How does her dream help her trap the real thieves?

POST-READING ACTIVITY:

1. Discuss the theme of honesty in this story. What does honesty mean to you? Can you think of other ways that Precious might have proven to the class that Poloko was innocent?

2. Discuss the theme of friendship in this story. Who acted as a true friend? What qualities do you look for in a friend? How can you tell when someone is a true friend?

3. Discuss the theme of stereotypes and what it means to judge people based on preconceived notions rather than evidence. Discuss the need to hear all sides of a story before you accuse a person of wrongdoing.

CURRICULUM CONNECTIONS:

1. Geography:

Draw a map of Africa and highlight the country of Botswana on the map. Locate the countries that are near Botswana on the map. What more do you want to know about Botswana after reading *The Great Cake Mystery*?

http://www.botswanatourism.co.bw/

2. Science/Biology—The Animal Kingdom:

Find information about the indigenous monkeys in Botswana. How does this information help you understand the story better?

http://www.wildlife-pictures-online.com/vervet-monkey-information.html

3. Language Arts:

Write a character sketch of your favorite character in the story. What do you think that character does in his or her spare time? What is your character's family like? Write a story of your own that includes the character you have chosen.

Look up information about the author of *The Great Cake Mystery*:

http://www.randomhouse.com/features/mccallsmith/main.php

4. Social Studies:

In the American judicial system, an accused person is "innocent until proven guilty." Discuss the meaning of this phrase. Research the history of the American Bill of Rights and how it came to be adopted by our Congress:

http://www.americaslibrary.gov/jb/nation/jb_nation_bofright_1.html

How do the laws of Botswana compare to the American system?

Discussion Guide prepared by Connie Rockman, Youth Literature Consultant, adjunct professor of children's and young adult literature, and editor of the H. W. Wilson *Junior Book of Authors and Illustrators* series.

Precious's Sponge Cake Worth Stealing

Ingredients
5 eggs (medium to large, but not jumbo)
1 cup very fine sugar
1 tablespoon vanilla extract
2 teaspoons fresh lemon juice
¾ cup flour
1 teaspoon salt

1 9-inch tube pan

Separate the eggs and beat the yolks in a mixing bowl until they are a bright-lemon color. Add the sugar gradually and continue beating until the mixture forms ribbons when the spoon is held above the bowl. Then add the vanilla and lemon. Beat the egg whites into the yolk mixture, then alternate, sifting some of the flour and salt into the batter. Continue to fold and sift in the flour until it is used up. Spoon the batter into a 9-inch ungreased tube pan with false bottom. It is important for sponge cake to adhere to the walls of the pan. Set in a preheated 350° oven for 40 minutes. Remove the pan from the oven and immediately place it facedown on a wire rack and let the cake hang for about 40 minutes before setting it upright again. This process keeps the cake from collapsing during the cooling period and also holds the texture of the cake. Remove the cake from the pan and place it in a tin that is not completely airtight, otherwise sweat will develop. Sponge cake is best cut with a serrated knife, using a sawing motion, or pulled apart with two table forks.

From THE TASTE OF COUNTRY COOKING by Edna Lewis. Copyright 2006 by Alfred A. Knopf, a division of Random House, Inc.

THE NO. 1 LADIES' DETECTIVE AGENCY SERIES

**"A literary confection....
There is no end to the pleasure."**
—The New York Times Book Review

Precious's dream of becoming a detective does come true
when she grows up. She opens the first ladies' detective agency in
Botswana. Read the adventures of her No. 1 Ladies' Detective Agency.

**The No. 1 Ladies' Detective
Agency**—Volume 1

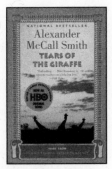

Tears of the Giraffe—
Volume 2

Morality for Beautiful Girls—
Volume 3

**The Kalahari Typing School
for Men**—Volume 4

The Full Cupboard of Life—
Volume 5

**In the Company of Cheerful
Ladies**—Volume 6

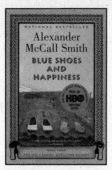

Blue Shoes and Happiness
Volume 7

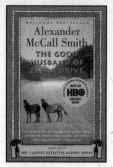

**The Good Husband of
Zebra Drive**—Volume 8

**The Miracle at Speedy
Motors**—Volume 9

**Tea Time for the
Traditionally Built**—Volume 10

**The Double Comfort
Safari Club**—Volume 11

**The Saturday Big Tent
Wedding Party**—Volume 12

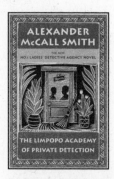

**The Limpopo Academy of
Private Detection**—Volume 13

More Books You Might Enjoy

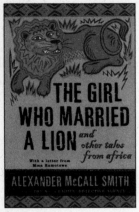

THE GIRL WHO MARRIED A LION
by Alexander McCall Smith

Gathered here is a beguiling selection of folktales from Zimbabwe and Botswana.

A girl discovers that her young husband might actually be a lion in disguise, but not before they have two sons who might actually be cubs. When a child made of wax follows his curiosity outside into the heat of daylight and melts, his siblings shape him into a bird with feathers made of leaves that enable him to fly into the light. Talking hyenas, milk-giving birds, and mysterious forces that reside in the landscape—these wonderful fables bring us the wealth, the variety, and the particular magic of traditional African lore.

978-0-375-42312-3 (Hardcover)
978-0-375-42344-4 (eBook)

CHIKE AND THE RIVER
by Chinua Achebe

"A straightforward African growing-up tale, and one told with a rare honesty.... A respectful, loving story."
—*San Francisco Chronicle*

Chinua Achebe, one of the world's most beloved and admired storytellers, tells the story of eleven-year-old Chike who longs to cross the Niger River to the city of Asaba, but he doesn't have money to pay for the ferry ride. With the help of his friend S.M.O.G., he embarks on a series of adventures to help him get there. Once he finally makes it across the river, Chike realizes that life on the other side is far different from his expectations, and he must find the courage within him to make it home.

978-0-307-47386-8 (Paperback)
978-0-307-74207-0 (eBook)